To my family
Who has always made Christmas special

Today is the day, Christmas is here
Around the world, Children wake up with cheer

Boxes and gifts
Packages and bows
Cookies and milk
Santa always knows

Now don't get us wrong
We love Christmas, too
But we've worked so hard,
We've gotten holes in our shoes

But here comes a secret
That no ones known until now
It's what happens after
Christmas-
You're about to find out

Santa, our boss
We know you know who
The beard, the laugh
The big guy, the red suit

He gives us a present
The gift of relaxation
A break from the hustle and
bustle
We get a vacation

A week to take off
Rest up for next year
Relax with our families
Get our minds clear

Norm likes to stay close
Where he likes to fish
He bundles up tight
Salmon are his wish

Sandy goes camping
Makes hot chocolate and s'mores
Lays in his hammock
Reads good books galore

Emma goes warmer
She relaxes in the sand
Makes a family of sandmen
Listens to reggae bands

Caleb loves sports
And baseball is his game
Hot dogs and peanuts
That's how he spends his days

Donald dives deep
It's how he spends his time
Scuba and snorkeling
It's his way to unwind

Vera gets a rush
She likes the wind in her hair
Water skis on her feet
You can find her out there

But after a week
We start to feel sad
We miss the North Pole
So we start to head back

And get back to business
Of making Christmas toys
For Santa to deliver
To all good girls and boys!

CPSIA information can be obtained
at www.ICGtesting.com
Printed in the USA
LVHW071952300919
632703LV00003B/58/P